I0750446

# THE GIRL FROM BENNIA STATION

NICKY PENTTILA

978-1-943192-53-3



A

Formatted with Vellum

# THE GIRL FROM BENNIA STATION

THE MORNING'S first rush hit hard. Pretty, clean, distracted grownups stampeding toward one of the twenty-four waiting rooms that would shuffle them onto the one of the big elevators that went all the way up to Bennia's orbital station. In the soaring off-world transit entry hall, empty in the middle except for the thick round pillars that held up the sky window ceiling, the commuters created their own wind. Today's breeze was fake vanilla and too much ozone, the scent of the air recyclers working overtime. Hot outside already, then, though the second sun hadn't even risen yet.

Aino pressed her back against one of the brushed-metal pillars, feeling the subtle vibration of the mag-lev trains thundering through the tubes fifty meters below. The comforting thrum traveled up through her worn boots, through her bones, into her soul, a machine heartbeat she'd known since she was small enough to hide behind these same pillars.

Around her, the bright oval room stretched in a blur of movement and chrome. Above her, one of the many departure boards flickered amber and blue, catching people's attention, drawing it away from Aino. The soaring archways and arty geometric patterns etched above them into the walls might as well have been wallpaper; background noise for her eyes. She'd mapped every service tunnel, every blind spot in the security cameras, every place where the flow naturally funneled people close together.

This was her hunting ground, familiar as breathing. Everything a predictable blur, like running water, until a likely suspect appeared.

The woman in the fancy forest-green pantsuit, her hair falling into her eyes, came into focus like she was the only one in color when the rest of the world was black and white.

Aino's gaze locked onto the delicate chain bracelet circling the woman's right wrist, catching the enhanced daylight. Real silver, not the synthetic stuff. The links looked hand-forged, irregular in that way that screamed expensive. Best, it was loose, sliding up and down as the woman poked impatiently at her wristcom, demanding something from it that it clearly wasn't giving. The crowd behind her was pushing her forward despite herself.

The roar of the terminal—nonstop announcements echoing off distant walls, thousands of feet stomping in reinforced magnetic boots, thousands of conversations mashing together—all of it faded to a whisper. Aino could hear the woman's irritated sigh, the soft click of green-manicured nails against the wristcom's surface, even the faint jingle of that bracelet as it shifted against the woman's wrist bones.

Aino straightened, letting her shoulders slump forward just so, making herself smaller. She scrubbed at her eyes with the back of her hand and let her lower lip tremble slightly. She put on her lost-kid face as fast as snapping her fingers—blonde hair floating around her face in the kind of tangled, innocent way that made grownups want to help.

This wasn't going to work for much longer, Sal the Fence kept telling her. She was getting too tall, too teen-gawky. But it was working for now. She'd think about tomorrow later.

Aino stumbled forward, timing her approach for the moment when the woman's attention was fully absorbed by her wristcom. The crowd parted around them like water around a boulder, everyone too focused on their own urgent destinations to notice one little girl bumping into a distracted businesswoman.

"Ope! Sorry, sorry!" Aino pitched her voice high and thin, the way adults expected kids to sound when they were overwhelmed. She steadied herself against the woman's arm, her fingers working with practiced precision. The bracelet's clasp popped at her touch like it wanted to be free.

"It's fine, sweetheart," the woman said absently, already turning away, her cinnamon scent lingering, as Aino mumbled another sorry and melted back into the crowd.

She held the bracelet a shade too long, crumpled up in her fist. It felt so nice on her palm, warmed by another person's pulse. The snatch always made her giddy, but almost immediately her hands started to shake with the post-giddies. The excitement wore off so fast now.

And she was still holding the stupid bracelet. She should have dropped it into her front pocket before the woman had even had a chance to talk. She jammed her whole hand into the pocket.

Let go.

The lady had called her sweetheart.

If only she was a sweetheart.

It was better to lift stuff from the mean, angry

people, not the nicer ones. But the nicer ones were easier.

Inside her pocket, her hand would not let go.

Her pocket was otherwise empty. First score of the day, it meant she could eat tonight, and maybe tomorrow.

Go with the flow.

The woman hadn't made it halfway across the room. Still distracted, still poking at her wristcom. She was going to miss her ride.

She was not going to miss the bracelet, until too late.

She was one of the ones with long hair, almost to her shoulders, so she didn't have a spacer job. Most commuters worked in the manufactories; lots of stuff could be made better in no gravity, or in vacuum. More than thirty thousand people went up and down the elevators each day, more than four times the number of folks who actually lived up there. Lots of space in space.

Lots of opportunity, for Aino. People who would never call her sweetheart.

Not worth it. This was the first rush. Plenty of other distracted rich folks to pick from today.

Aino started drifting with the current of commuters toward the woman in green. She still looked bright against the black and gray crowd.

"Scuse? You dropped this?" Aino's traitor hand

was holding the bracelet, not crumpled up for safety but stretched all out.

She woman gasped as she recognized the bracelet. "My stars!" She grabbed Aino's other arm.

Aino froze. Now *she* was the boulder in the river. Was she a cop?

The woman took the bracelet in her other hand.

"Bless you," she said as she leaned close to Aino. She kissed Aino's forehead, close to her eye. Then she let her go, and swirled away.

Aino still could not move. The woman's lips had shocked her like those shitty security sticks.

She couldn't remember when she'd last been kissed.

She lifted her hand up to the spot, but didn't touch it.

Didn't want to wipe it off.

Wonderful.

Suddenly, she felt dizzy. She didn't know what day it was. Her stomach growled. Everything was out of whack.

She wasn't good for anything like this. She surfed the forward flow and made it to the side of the room. Against the white walls and windows sat fake-wood benches, the kind with armrests so that grownups couldn't lie down. Maybe someone had left half a cup of joe, or a juice.

The bench sat along the way to Gate 12 and the

outer docks. The biggest crowd at the moment, waiting for the nest-soonest climber car. The woman had been headed to Gate 10, so she must have had to race to make her ride.

Sure enough, a steaming cup of something sat on the bench down the way. Smelled like burnt almonds and fake energy. Aino shifted smoothly against the tide and settled next to the flimsy cup, making herself a ghost again. Just another kid waiting for transport, invisible to the cameras until all the tall folks were gone.

The bench was hard. She missed her mom. And her dad, too. Well, they'd be back in two years, assuming they didn't mess up the indenture, or get in some other trouble. Then the company would give them all their papers back, and Aino would be a citizen again, instead of an undocumented alien.

Two years.

If they even could come back. They were too far out for messages, apparently, even text-based ones.

*You'll be fine, baby. Remember what I showed you.*

And she was.

For now.

That's when she heard them.

"—forgot we had to wait until after commute. Damn waste of time."

"Mebbe not."

Two voices—spacer accents. Not a lot of them

waited around here. Most stayed in the two bars out by the spacer part of the terminal.

The echoes in this place created strange pockets where sound bounced in unexpected ways, and Aino had learned to listen for conversations that weren't meant to be overheard. She glanced around. They must be the ones in scruffy jackets and non-matching tough pants. Spacer buzz cuts.

"We could look around," the man said. He tapped the ankle resting on his opposite knee.. "For that Kellerman girl."

"The runaway?" The woman, closer, was leaning forward, elbows on knees. Her face looked beat-up, but the short hair made the shape of her head look beautiful.

"Lost, they said. Field trip, missed the shuttle home. She was here, in the terminal, two days ago."

"Two days?" the woman looked at the man. "You know where she is, then."

"Maybe not. She's simple, or something." The man's hair was like shorn straw, his eyes round and blue. "Traffickers wouldn't want her."

Traffickers. They had a look, her mom had showed her first thing. Aino was best at being invisible from them—make a hard face, scowl, stand next to someone big. She hadn't seen any of those types in a while, though. The security cameras could pick them out as easily as she could.

Except that one woman, but Aino hadn't seen her around, either.

Aino started to scan the edges of the building. This girl, if she made it to the toilets, could find plenty of places to hide. Closets, access panels to the water pipes and blowers and ladders down to more noisy stuff.

But why would a girl like her need to hide?

"Station's getting pressure from base command, I heard. Kellermans are mega-connected."

"Good luck," the woman said. "I'm sure there's been search party. We'll never find her."

"Vera, you said you wanted to get on-base, right? Here's your chance."

The woman sat up straight. Started looking around, at the swirl of moving grownups. "What's she look like, again?"

"Pale blonde hair, blue eyes, real pretty the way kids can be. Small for her age—looks more like eight than twelve."

Aino's breath caught. Her heart lit on fire. They could be describing her. She gripped the worn-smooth armrest with both hands as if it was about to run off, and closed her eyes so she could hear better.

"What's she wearing?"

The man paused, maybe looking it up. "Pink synth-silk dress."

Ice water ran down Aino's spine. She glanced down at her worn clothes—faded blue tunic and leggings. Both were smooth and shiny, but with wear, not because they were silk.

But her hair was exactly that shade of pale blonde, and her face had that same forgettable prettiness that made adults' eyes slide right past her.

"There's a reward," the man's voice was fading, like he knew he was losing his audience.

"Lucky for somebody."

Aino, still in her forget-me pose, sat feet dangling on the bench, her mind alight.

The orbital station. Where the elevator required real identification and big money, neither of which she had. But these spacers—they'd have their own shuttle, wouldn't they? Fast, direct, no security checks.

The station was good pickings, Sal the Fence said. Sal had lived there until she'd been kicked off for lifting the wrong person's bag. The station had access tunnels, hidden panels everywhere. Too much crime in the important places to afford to send even one cop to patrol the stray corridors or inside the big utility tunnels.

Best, the food places and snack carts always needed workers, and didn't always ask for ID. Wouldn't matter that she was getting taller, if she had a real job.

All she had to do was turn herself into a lost little girl named Kellerman.

Aino took a shaky breath and let her shoulders curve inward, making herself smaller. She messed up her hair and pinched her cheeks pink until they hurt, then bit down on her lower lip hard enough to make her eyes water. The pain would really sell it.

She drooped her head, letting her blond curls sway past the sides of her face. She could still see them from the corner of her eyes. The man was facing her, but looking up, at one of the departure boards.

Aino sighed loudly like a sad wounded animal. The man's gaze dropped to her, and then back to the board again.

And then back to her.

He launched off his bench and rushed over to her. He was tall, and fast. Going down on his knees, he tried to look at her face. He smelled like coal but his eyes were kind.

And hopeful.

Aino's heart was pounding loud enough that everyone in the whole terminal must be able to hear it. A tremor started in her left knee—the same stupid shake that always gave her away when she was really scared—and she had to lock her leg straight to stop it.

"What's your name, sweetheart?" His voice had gone gentle, careful.

"Em...ma." The lie came out higher than she'd planned, her voice cracking on the last syllable like she was some little kid instead of almost-thirteen. She swallowed hard, tasting copper at the back of her throat. Her fingernails dug crescents into her palms, using the sharp pain to keep the panic down where it belonged.

The woman, shorter but thicker, had drifted closer. Unlike the man, whose face showed growing excitement and relief, this one watched Aino with calculating eyes. She felt her gaze like a scanner, taking in details: the way she held herself, the quality of her worn clothes, the practiced nature of her distress.

Their eyes met for just a moment, and she saw something flicker there—recognition, but not the kind the man showed. Hers was like when you saw another kid who knows the same tricks you do.

The hair on Aino's arms stood up.

"Emma Kellerman," the tall spacer repeated, shaking his wristcom to turn it on. "Your parents have been so worried."

"Scared," Aino whispered. She let real exhaustion creep into her voice—it wasn't hard to find. She shouldn't talk much. She didn't know what her accent was but it sure wasn't spacer. Or orbital.

"Marcus," the shorter spacer said quietly, "we should get her to the ship. Poor kid's been through enough without standing around in this chaos."

Marcus. Now she had a name for the mark. The other one was the one she'd have to watch.

"Right, absolutely." Marcus was already moving, his protective instincts fully engaged. "I'm Marcus and this is Vera. We're going to take you home to your family, okay?"

Aino nodded, still not meeting their eyes directly.

Marcus stood up and stepped away, his attention on his wristcom. "I'm requesting emergency permission to leave."

Vera held a hand out to Aino. Her hand was calloused and warm. Pulling Aino to her feet, Vera leaned down close to Aino's ear.

"Smart," she said. "Showing just what people expect to see."

Aino's step faltered for just a moment before she caught herself. She looked up at Vera, trying to read her intentions in her weathered face. Aino said nothing, just let her eyes widen slightly—the look of a child who didn't understand what the adult meant.

Vera smiled—not the gentle, reassuring smile Marcus had been giving her, but something sharper, more appreciative. "Don't worry, kid.

Sometimes we all need a little help to get where we're going."

---

THE SHUTTLE'S airlock sealed behind them with a soft pneumatic hiss, and Aino fought the dizziness. Everything about this space felt alien, dangerous. The gray-blue walls curved inward like being inside a metal egg, and the air tasted of recycled oxygen and old tires, cleaner than the terminal but somehow more artificial, as if each breath had been scrubbed of anything remotely organic.

Cargo shuttle, obviously. Only this little apple slice up-front was for people. The only windows were the ones in front of the two seats for Marcus and Vera, but Aino didn't see how they'd have time to look out the windows, with all those monitors and knobs and dials and buttons and trackpads and stick-things on the table in front of them.

Vera was sealing the inner door, but Marcus was already in his chair. She could tell it was his because it didn't have a box underneath to help him reach all the dials and knobs. Vera's did, and it also had a bar to rest her feet.

"Sit anywhere, Emma," Marcus said. Aino startled at the name. Luckily, Marcus was looking at his part of the table and not paying her any attention.

Along the sides of the shuttle there were two benches that looked like they could be beds; in the middle, four bucket-seat chairs, two by two, sat in rows right behind Marcus and Vera.

Aino stared at the chairs, her mind racing. She couldn't tell if it was hot in here or if she was burning up from the inside. The chairs all looked the same—gray padding with complex seat belts hanging loose like complicated spider webs. How was she supposed to know which one? Did it matter? Were there rules about where children sat?

She chose the seat closest to Marcus, figuring that was the safest spot in a crash. The cushion felt strange beneath her—too soft and springy, like sitting on a pillow filled with air. When she tried to pull the harness straps over her shoulders, they twisted in ways that made no sense. The webbing felt wrong under her fingers—too smooth, too synthetic, nothing like the rough fiber cables and worn fabric she was used to.

The seat was a trap. Too soft, too yielding. Her body kept sinking into cushions that felt like quicksand after years of hard benches and metal floors. She couldn't find her balance, couldn't feel solid beneath her. At the terminal, she always knew exactly how surfaces would respond to her weight, which pipes would hold her, which grates would give way. This chair lied to her body with every shift.

The harness had buckles and adjusters that seemed designed for someone with three extra hands. Each time she thought she had it right, another strap would slip or twist. Her practiced fingers, so sure when picking locks or pockets, fumbled stupidly with these stupid straps. Heat burned up her chest, through her neck, into her face. She had to bite down on the swear word about to come out of her mouth.

"Here, let me help with that," Marcus said, reaching over. But before he could get too close, Vera appeared at Aino's shoulder.

"I got it," Vera said smoothly. "Harnesses are tricky for kids. Emma here probably hasn't been on many cargo carriers, have you?"

Aino shook her head gratefully as Vera's experienced hands sorted out the straps. But she caught the meaningful look Vera shot her a look that said, *I know you don't know what you're doing*.

"Orbital control knows we're bringing Emma home?" Vera asked as she settled into her chair.

Emma. She had to remember that was her.

"Yep," Marcus said. "Hope they drop the finder's fee in our account right away. I hear there's good eats on-base."

"If they even let us on-base." Vera sounded bitter. "You remember last time?

"Last time, we reeked." Marcus turned to smile at Vera. "Glimmerantin beans, remember?"

Vera rolled her eyes and turned back to whatever she was doing. "How could I ever forget?"

"This time, we got a prize. Bet they put us in Bay One."

Vera leaned forward, punching buttons and screens like a pro. But Aino noticed tension in her shoulders, a tight set to her jaw. Something else was up.

"Base communications, this shuttle Peregrine X," Vera spoke into her headset. "Requesting priority approach clearance. We have the missing Kellerman child aboard."

Static crackled from the speakers, followed by an officious voice: "Copy that, Peregrine. Standby for clearance confirmation."

While Vera dealt with the base, Marcus busied himself with pre-flight checks. Aino tried to watch without being obvious, but every beep and hum from the shuttle's systems made her jump. The seat beneath her began to warm up—apparently that was normal, from Marcus's casual lack of concern—and she felt a subtle vibration through the hull that might have been engines powering up or the whole ship about to shake apart.

Nothing like the cozy vibration of the mag-lev trains.

"Comms are shitheads," Vera muttered, adjusting something on her screen with increasing frustration. "Trying to patch through to station personnel directory."

Aino caught fragments of Vera's side conversations as she worked through various communication channels. Something about reaching someone in "Environmental Systems" and then "Can you transfer me to Dr. Chen in the research division?" Each attempt seemed to hit dead ends or busy signals.

"All passengers secure?" Marcus called back. "We're cleared for departure in thirty seconds."

Aino gripped her armrests, knuckles white beneath her pale skin. The vibration was getting stronger, and she could hear what sounded like a metal whirlpool spinning up somewhere way behind her back. Was this normal? Emma Kellerman would know, probably. Emma would have done this dozens of times, traveling between the orbital base and the surface for school trips and vacations.

"First time?" Vera asked quietly, still wearing her headset but with one ear free.

Aino nodded.

"Launch is the worst part," Vera said. "Marcus

makes it easy. After that, it's just floating. Like being in a very boring, very expensive elevator."

"Launching in ten," Marcus announced. "Everyone hold on."

Great stars above! She was going into space!

First came the noise, a roar like an angry mega-monster was hurtling toward her from behind.

Then, what felt like a mega-monster's giant hand punched Aino deep into her seat. A whimper escaped before she could stop it—a small, pathetic sound that would have gotten her mocked in the tunnels. Her hands clutched the armrests so hard her knuckles went white, then numb. She couldn't stop her teeth from chattering, even though she wasn't cold. When her stomach lurched, she had to clench her jaw shut to keep from throwing up.

Then the shuttle shuddered around then, the monster shaking it hard. On a small screen on the desk she caught a glimpse of the planet's surface falling away at impossible speed—buildings shrinking to dots, then patches of brown and green terrain, then the curve of the world itself.

Then the roaring stopped, and she could hear the clicks and beeps of the front panels again.

But now her sense of balance went completely haywire. Up and down became meaningless words. Her stomach dropped and then seemed to keep falling, as if someone had cut all the strings holding her organs in place. Her brain kept insisting the shuttle was tumbling end over end, but her eyes said they were flying straight.

The saliva in her mouth felt wrong. Thick and clingy, pooling strangely against her teeth instead of flowing like it should. When she swallowed, the liquid seemed to take forever to go down, floating in her throat like it couldn't decide which direction was down either. Her tongue had swollen up.

Every survival instinct she'd ever developed was screaming contradictory warnings. The part of her brain that always knew which way to fall, which way to run, where to put her weight—that part went silent, leaving her floating, terrified, alone.

She tried to grip the armrests even tighter, but her hands felt disconnected from her arms. The pressure in her head built and built until her ears popped with a sharp crack that made her gasp. Her vision grayed at the edges, and she couldn't tell if it was from fear or from her body's complete confusion about which way the blood should flow.

"Welcome to zero-g," Marcus said cheerfully. "Flight time, fifty minutes. How are you doing back there, Emma?"

She flinched at the name, but less than last time.

"I know, I know," said Marcus. "The super-shuttles take ten. Even the elevator's only thirty." He must have thought her wince was for the extra time? "But that just means you get to spend more quality time with us."

Aino opened her mouth to answer and discovered she didn't trust her stomach enough to speak. She nodded weakly instead.

"She's fine," Vera said, catching her eye in the reflection of a dark monitor screen.

Vera, on the other hand, was not. She kept calling and calling, her voice getting more strained by the minute.

"Base personnel directory, this is Vera Santos on shuttle Peregrine. I need to reach Dr. Lin Chen, priority personal message."

"Dr. Chen is currently in meetings," came the tinny response. "I can take a message."

"Tell her Vera's coming up. Tell her I need five minutes. Tell her..." Vera's voice dropped, but in the shuttle's confined space, Aino could still hear. "Tell her I kept my part of the bargain."

The silence that followed felt heavy with unfinished business. Marcus stopped humming and turned to look at Vera, puzzlement on his face.

"Wait," he said. "Vera, why are you trying to reach Lin? Last month you were complaining about how she was making your life miserable, keeping you grounded with all her bureaucratic games."

Vera's hands stilled on the communication

panel. For a moment, Aino thought she wouldn't answer.

"She has something that belongs to me," Vera said finally. "My genetic passport for the outer colonies."

"Your what?" Marcus turned in his seat to face her fully. "I thought those were issued by Cooperative Health Authority."

"They are. But Lin was the examining physician for my compatibility screening two years ago. She's the one who signed off on my genetic markers—radiation resistance, bone density, all the bio requirements for deep space work. She cleared me."

Vera's voice went flat. "When I… when things fell apart between us, she agreed to release the passport if I stayed away from the base. No contact, no visits, no messages through mutual friends."

Aino had heard it before. Just like what happened to her parents. Somebody else got to decide everything—where they went, what they did, when they could leave. Her mom used to say they were "contractually obligated," but Aino knew what that really meant. It meant owned. It meant you couldn't just run when things got bad.

At least Vera was fighting for her freedom instead of just accepting whatever was decided for her.

"And you agreed to that?" Marcus sounded like he didn't believe her.

"What choice did I have? She could have flagged my results as inconclusive, made me start the whole screening process over with a different doc. Another six-month wait, minimum. Another chunk of change I don't have." Vera put a foot up on the edge of the table and slouched, rubbing her hands through the short hairs on her head. She knocked the headset off, but didn't seem to care.

So the doctor lady could mess up Vera's paperwork on purpose. Make her do everything all over again. Like when the food line monitors said your ration card was "invalid" just because they didn't like your face.

"I kept my end of the bargain for eighteen months," Vera said. "Stayed planetside, took the pathetic in-system runs, didn't even try to contact her."

"So what changed?"

Vera was quiet for so long that Aino thought she wouldn't answer. When she finally spoke, her voice was barely above the soft hum of the shuttle.

"I'm tired of being trapped. Tired of the same routes, same stations, same small life. The outer colonies are the only place left where you can still find something new, something that hasn't been mapped and catalogued and regulated to death."

She looked up, out the dark windows. "The passport is mine. I earned it. And I'm done waiting for her to decide when I deserve my freedom."

So that's why Vera had been so willing to help with Aino's con. She had to get to the base, to get something that belonged to her but someone else wouldn't give her. Like when the older kids took your food and held it over your head, making you jump for it, and then ate it right in front of you anyway. Except this was way worse, because it was grown-ups doing it and you couldn't fight them.

Marcus was silent for a while. Then: "Why'd you break up, anyway?"

"Seriously?"

"Right, right, sorry." He waved a hand in front of him like he was trying to erase his stupid words.

But Vera answered him anyway. "Usual reason. She wanted kids. I didn't. She said she'd wasted her fertile window on me. I said you're welcome." She banged her head on the back of her chair, closed her eyes, and sighed like all the air was leaving her for good.

Marcus shook his head. He scratched the back of his neck. Nothing he could say about that. He glanced back at Aino.

"We'll be docking in about ten minutes. Feeling better?"

Aino nodded, though her stomach still felt unsettled. "Tablet? Text my parents?"

"Of course! Should've thought of that." Marcus reached into a storage compartment and pulled out a slim device. "Here, this one has the base directory and some educational programs loaded, too. My kid left it, last time they were here. Was just waiting for you."

Aino accepted the tablet gratefully, her fingers already working to navigate to the station schematics. She'd studied every public blueprint she could find of the orbital base, memorizing the basic layout and dreaming of escape. But now she could see the real thing—service corridors, maintenance shafts, and most importantly, the route from the arrival concourse down to the lower residential and work levels where she could disappear. Now where was Bay One?

She hoped Vera's doctor would be there to meet them. Nothing like grownups fighting to make everyone miss the kid slipping into the shadows.

---

THEY DIDN'T GET to go to Bay One, which was a fancy one, where the shuttles could fly right in and land, not have to hook up with the floaty-tubes and bob around outside the station like caught fish.

But they did get to latch onto one of the floaty-tube fish hooks just past Bay One. Which was huge—as big as the whole of the transit station down below.

Which was only right, because the station itself was huger than huge. A fat white cylinder with windows or doors that that looked like holes, it looked like one of those wheels of cheese they put in shop windows during the winter holidays. Only ginormous.

She knew the place was big, of course. But the moons were bigger, everyone said, and the moons were too small for living on. Which, now she thought of it, didn't make sense. The station was beautiful and shiny and lumpy and terrifying and absolutely nothing like the simple schematics she'd been studying on the tablet.

They landed near the center of one of the broad sides of the wheel. Here, gravity was light, growing stronger as you moved outward toward the rim. Most people lived in comfort close to the outer rings, while the manufactories occupied the low-gravity inner zones closer to the wheel's core. The orbital elevators connected almost precisely at the middle radius. They'd docked only a few floaty-tubes away from one of the two elevators—so the first commute must be done.

"Welcome back to Bennia Station, Emma," Marcus said, powering down the shuttle's systems.

"They put us way close, dock set two. Should be no time at all before we get you to your parents."

Aino's stomach clenched. They weren't going to meet her parents. Or Emma's. More like a pack of security goons who would be standing around wondering why everyone was lying. Aino glanced at the tablet in her lap, quickly memorizing the route from the main corridor of dock set two to the nearest maintenance access point—a service hatch that connected to the vertical transport shafts with stairs leading to the lower levels. Second choice, just past that, a hatch that went she wasn't sure where.

"Need help?" Vera asked Aino, looking at her harness as Vera slipped out of her own. Aino shook her head. It took her no time to undo all the seat restraints. Show her something once, and she had it down.

But she wasn't ready to get out of the seat just yet. She let Vera pass, to do whatever to the door hatches, and pocketed the tablet. Marcus finished with the knobs and buttons, and popped himself out of his harness. He straightened his wrinkled jacket, and then held out a hand to her.

She took it, and he gently pulled her to her feet.

"No reason to be scared now," he said. He was so nice. Too bad his smile made him look a little scary.

One door cycled open, and then the second. Immediately, the base's atmosphere rushed in—warmer than the shuttle, but wrong somehow. Fizzy, like they'd scrubbed out everything that made air real. No trace of food or sweat or life, just the sharp bite of whatever chemicals they used to kill germs. It made her nose itch.

Vera led the way, showing by slightly exaggerated example where Aino should place her feet when she stepped from the hard metal of the shuttle floor to the somewhat bouncy floor of the floaty tube. Which, now that she was inside, seemed much more solid than it looked from the outside. More like the arched hallways at the orphanage.

Aino shuddered. She was not going back there.

They stepped out into a room that looked like the main hall of the planetside terminal, if the planetside terminal had been built by engineers who hated people. The ceiling soared overhead, but instead of a window it was criss-crossed with pipes and cables and whatever else they needed to stay alive up here. Bright lights shone down from under the criss-crossed mess, but they didn't hide it from view.

Might be places to hide up there. But how would she even get there?

This floor felt wrong, but in a different way. At

the terminal, the mag-levs hummed up through the floor, through your bones, a warm throb. Here, the vibration was higher, thinner—more like a mosquito's whine than a heartbeat. It made her teeth ache.

The walls were some kind of composite that wasn't even pretending to be pretty. Even the echoes were wrong. Down below, sounds bounced and multiplied. Here, the acoustics were so perfect that every footstep landed clean and separate, like hammers on metal.

She could hear her own breathing, loud. Could hear *everyone's* breathing. The terminal's beautiful chaos of overlapping noise was gone, replaced by this terrible clarity where every sound stood out naked and exposed.

Holographic signs with lots of symbols instead of words floated at eye level, directing traffic this way and that.

But the good part was all the shadows. Gaps between structural supports where the overhead lighting didn't quite reach. Maintenance panels set into the walls at regular intervals, some of them slightly askew as if they hadn't been bolted in right after the last repair. Closed sliding doors marked with simple text instead of flashy holograms.

This was a place built by someone who didn't really care if it was pretty, just that it worked.

Good. Ugly places always had the best hiding spots.

"This way," Marcus said, guiding them toward one of the open doors, which had a big window in the wall next to it. People of all sorts looked out, waiting for whoever they were waiting for.

Nobody was waiting for her.

Aino felt the jiggle-leg start. The need to run. Hold on, she told her leg, just a little bit more. Just beyond that door was a storage room, and if she could get a little farther in, that access corridor.

Just inside the door was the checkpoint, where a small bored man in a brown uniform sat on a tall, four-legged stool, a scanner-tablet in his hand. In front of him was one of those walk-through scanner things. The scanners looked for bad germs and other stuff, but they didn't tell people who you were anymore. They'd made a law about that up here.

Almost there.

The officer's stool had no wear marks on the legs. How long had he been sitting there? Everything looked like it had been installed yesterday. Her fingers itched for something familiar to touch. A wall with texture, a surface that showed human use.

Vera walked on Aino's other side, but her attention was elsewhere. Her eyes kept scanning the crowd behind the window, searching faces. She'd barely spoken since they'd docked. Tension radiating from her like heat.

"Name and purpose of visit?" The security officer looked bored as he gestured for them to walk through the arch.

"Marcus Chen and Vera Santos, returning with the missing Kellerman child," Marcus replied, producing his identification.

The scanner beeped green as each of them passed through, but Aino noticed how the officer's expression sharpened when he looked at her. "Emma Kellerman, age twelve, reported missing three days ago?"

"That's right," Marcus said. "We found her at the planetary terminal. Poor thing was hiding in the maintenance areas, too scared to ask for help."

The officer consulted his tablet, frowning slightly. "I'm showing family was notified of your approach, but..." He tapped the device, as if that might change whatever information it was displaying. "There's a slight delay. They're asking if you all could wait in the family services lounge while they make their way down from the residential sector." He looked up apologetically. "It's a long walk."

Aino's heart started to race. Her leg to jiggle. Her thoughts to sharpen.

The walk was not the problem.

She needed to cut loose. Now.

Once they were past the scanner, Vera's tension ratcheted up. She started staring at people's faces like they were lifelines in a snowstorm.

The hall was off-white, with a lot of shouty posters on the walls telling you what not to do. The long rectangle lights in the ceiling were too bright.

"Could I use the restroom?" she asked quietly, looking up at Marcus with what she hoped was innocent urgency. "I've been waiting."

"Of course, sweetheart. Vera, could you…"

"I'll take her," Vera said quickly. "There's one just a little further down."

Marcus nodded, and turned into a different hall, toward the family lounge, identified on the sign by an image of three people with circles for heads and triangle bodies clumped together.

As they walked away from the checkpoint, Aino saw the first of the doors, the closet. She let herself pass it. The maintenance access door would be better.

The artificial gravity felt weird, especially after the zero-g of the shuttle. Her legs weren't sure what force to set her feet down with, like when she had a fever and the room seemed to shrink and widen and shrink again.

No time for that. She could see the maintenance door, just past the door to the bathrooms.

Her fingers already knew the shape of the handle —horizontal bar, push down, no sound, slip through. Except her legs felt like they were moving through water. Each step took forever. The too-perfect floor was slippery under her worn boots, no grip, no texture, just that awful smoothness that made her feel like she was skating instead of running.

The hall was crowded with grownups moving in both directions, some angry walking superfast, some dawdling or reading all the posters. None even glanced at one apparent woman and child.

But Vera automatically put a protective hand on Aino's shoulder when a maintenance worker brushed past them with a loaded cart. "I'll wait here while you..."

But she didn't finish the sentence. Her attention had been caught by something else. A small woman in a blue doctor coat standing near a bank of departure and arrival screens, her dark hair pulled back in a severe bun.

"Lin," Vera breathed. The hand on Aino's shoulder gripped so tight Aino thought her collarbone would break.

The doctor turned at the sound of her name, and Aino saw her face go through a rapid series of expressions. surprise, anger, pain, resolve. She was younger than Aino had expected, but still had that stiff-relaxed posture of someone used to being the boss.

The doctor's gaze shifted to Aino, taking in her blonde hair and small frame. "And who's this?" Her voice was surprisingly low, like warm chocolate.

"Emma Kellerman," Vera said. "We found her at the planetside terminal. She got separated from her group."

Something flickered across Lin's face—confusion, then anger.

Aino's knees wobbled. It felt like the floor had dropped away. A wash of cold fear swept her, then hot shame, then cold again.

This was it.

She'd failed.

"No, it's not." She said it like she was mad at the lie. "I gave Emma her last medical clearance myself just last months." But she looked at Vera's hand, tight and protective on Aino's shoulder, and frowned.

The doctor's voice carried too well in this horrible space. Every word clear and separate, impossible to pretend nobody had heard. Aino could hear Vera's pulse in her throat, could hear the doctor's shifting her weight from foot to foot. Too much information, all of it sharp-edged.

She had to get out of here. The doc was going to

call the brown uniforms, and that would be it. Plus they were starting to get noticed. They were blocking the flow of traffic.

Aino leaned toward the far wall, where the maintenance door was, trying to move Vera subtly.

No joy.

"I kept my part of the bargain," Vera replied, moving closer to the doctor instead. Aino let her move, let the hand just slide off her shoulder. "Eighteen months, Lin. That's gotta be enough."

"And now you're breaking it." The doctor did that hands-on-hips thing like a pro.

"Because I need what's mine." Vera pointed her thumb at her own chest.

"I… I can't let you go."

Aino took a step backward, then another. Neither woman was paying attention to her anymore. They were locked in their own drama, complete with waving arms and jabbing fingers. Plus, they were attracting attention.

The service corridor beckoned, promising the shadows she needed to disappear into the base's inner guts. All she had to do was walk away, and become someone new in the vast underbelly of Bennia Station.

Behind her, she could hear Vera's voice, cracking: "Just give me the passport, babe. I'm already gone. Cut the strings."

Aino didn't wait to hear the answer. The maintenance door was unlocked. She slipped into the service corridor. And started to run.

Same boring hallway, more doors. Keypad locks next to each one. Door two, air circulation. Three, door controls. Four, lower levels—yes!

But it was locked.

Aino's fingers punched the access panel next to the door, but the simple numeric pad might as well have been written in calculus. The first stupid pad with a code that was not one of the basic five patterns her mom had taught her before she could read.

Blasted engineers, make stuff so hard. The keypad was cold under her fingers, each button giving that soft little click that meant nothing, told her nothing. At the terminal, she could feel which buttons were worn down from use, could guess at common codes from the oil patterns. Here every button felt identical—untouched, unused, or cleaned so often it didn't matter. Even the numbers glowed that horrible steady blue, not flickering like proper electronics should.

Her heart beat in her throat, so loud she could hear the echo. The first beat in her inner ears, then in the outer air. Her breaths came so fast she wasn't sure any air was even getting in.

She tugged down on the gray metal latch. Nothing.

She had to get through this door.

Or another one.

She tried door three. "Door controls" sounded good.

The lock didn't click.

Behind her, she could hear footsteps—measured, unhurried, the sound of adults who knew exactly where she was because there was nowhere else to go. The corridor turned their voices into weapons, bouncing clear and sharp off walls that refused to muffle anything. She could hear Vera's breathing, tight and controlled. Could hear the whisper of Lin's coat against her legs. Could hear a wristcom beeping—Marcus's song? Probably another message about the real Emma.

The walls pressed in around her, smooth painted-metal surfaces that sucked heat from her body without giving anything back. Not like the terminal's pillars that held warmth from all the bodies pressed against them. These walls were vampires, stealing what little warmth she had left. The air tasted thin, and metallic, nothing like the thick soup of smells she was used to navigating by. How did people find their way when everything smelled like nothing?

The hum behind the air-circulation door seemed

to grow louder, harsher, like the base itself was closing in on her.

She tried another panel, frantically pressing combinations that might work—1234, 0000, 1111—knowing even as she did it that these security systems weren't going to be fooled by children with desperate fingers. The display just blinked red, red, red.

Her fingers had gone clumsy and thick, like she was wearing gloves. She couldn't make them hit the right buttons anymore. A hot pressure built behind her eyes. No, no, no, she wasn't going to cry, she never cried, only on purpose, random crying was for babies and marks—but her vision blurred anyway. She scrubbed at her eyes angrily, hating the wetness on her cheeks, hating how her breath kept hitching in these stupid little gasps that made her sound exactly like what she was: a scared kid with nowhere left to run.

"Nowhere to run," The doctor's voice carried clearly down the corridor, calm and professional. Not unkind, but final. "The service tunnels all require biometric clearance. And there are cameras everywhere, not like down-planet."

Aino pressed herself against the cool metal wall, her mind racing through options that dwindled with each passing second. The ceiling was too high to reach, the floor too solid to break through. Even if she could find an air vent—and the ones she could see were barely large enough for cleaning drones—where would it lead? This wasn't the rambling, chaotic structure of the planetside terminal with its forgotten corners and overlooked spaces. This was an orbital station where every cubic meter was planned, monitored, accounted for.

"Emma?" Marcus's voice cracked with confusion. He must have followed the sound of Vera's commotion. "Emma! What's wrong?"

The sound of her fake name made something twist in Aino's chest. Marcus had been kind to her, genuinely concerned for a lost child's welfare. He didn't deserve to be caught up in her deception, but here he was, probably thinking she was having some kind of breakdown from trauma.

"That's not Emma," Lin said, and Aino heard Marcus's sharp intake of breath.

"What?" His footsteps quickened. "But… but she knew about being lost, about the educational trip…"

"Anyone could have overheard those details at the terminal." Lin's voice was getting closer. "The question is who this child really is, and why you brought her aboard."

Aino tried one more access panel, her fingers clumsy as she pressed the codes. The red blink slapped her hard. She sagged against the wall. All her years of survival instincts had hit their limit. There was nowhere left to run in this metal maze, nowhere to hide from people who belonged here when she so obviously didn't.

The corridor felt like it was shrinking, the ceiling pressing down, the walls closing in. This wasn't like the open spaces of the planetside terminal where she could blend into crowds and slip through forgotten gaps. Or run off to the river, and sit and think.

This was a closed system, and she was the bug that didn't belong.

"Lin, please," Vera's desperation felt contagious. "Just give me the passport. I'll take her back planetside. We'll all just get on with our lives."

Somebody's shadow hit Aino on the shoulder, and on the wall holding the keypad. Aino's leg jiggled so hard she collapsed to the floor.

Not getting out of this one.

"Why?" It was the doctor, Lin, her blue coat bright white under the harsh lighting. Vera, her face so full of feelings it looked swollen, had stopped a few steps away, along with Marcus.

"Why does this child matter so much to you?" Lin asked, stepping closer to Aino. "You've never shown interest in children before."

"She's just a kid who needed a hand—"

"No reward," Marcus was looking at a message on his wristcom. "Emma showed up this morning. She never left the base." He glared at Aino. "She must've heard us talking about the girl and saw an opportunity."

Lin stared at Aino like she was a particularly interesting specimen. Then she squatted down.

"Turn your hands over," she said quietly.

Aino's fists tightened reflexively. Her hands were weapons, tools, her life—but they were also evidence. Every mark told a story she didn't want read.

She forced her fingers to uncurl, knuckle by knuckle. The air cold against skin that was used to being hidden in pockets, clenched in fists. Her palms were mapped with tiny scars and calluses, the nails bitten down to nothing. A fresh scrape ran along one thumb—that stupid food dispenser near Waiting Room Ten.

Lin's fingers were impossibly soft, like she'd never scraped them raw on metal grating or cut them on broken glass. The doctor's touch was gentle but thorough, turning Aino's hands this way and that like she was reading a book. Her thumb traced the raised line of scar tissue along Aino's index finger—the one from the broken bottle when she was nine. Another fingertip found the callus ridge where she gripped ladders

"Malnutrition," Lin murmured, pressing lightly at the base of Aino's fingernails. "And these pressure marks..." She tapped one of the deep grooves worn into Aino's palms. "From gripping metal surfaces. Climbing?"

Aino's whole body went hot. She wanted to snatch her hands back, shove them deep in her pockets where they belonged. This woman was reading her whole life story from her skin—every desperate night, every hungry day, every time she'd had to fight or run or hide.

Lin's expression shifted, the stern professional giving way to something softer. "How old are you? Really?"

"Twelve." The word came out defensive. "Almost thirteen."

"When's your birthday?"

Aino's mouth opened, then closed. When was the last time anyone had asked? When was the last time it had mattered? "Springtime?"

Something passed across Lin's face—not pity exactly, but a kind of recognition.

Really?

Lin let Aino go, and stood up. She turned to look at Vera. "And you helped her. She could never have fooled you. You protected her, covered for her inexperience, got her here. Why?"

Aino slumped further down the wall, the cold

metal stealing warmth from her back through her thin clothes. She could hear the truth in Lin's words. Soon Vera would be angry too, would see Aino as just another problem that had cost her what she wanted most.

"You've never been protective of anyone," Lin continued, her voice softer now. "Not even me. But you were protecting her."

Vera was holding onto her chest like she was out of breath. "I don't know what you're trying to—"

"I'm trying to understand why a woman who told me she never wanted children, who said family was just another kind of cage, would risk everything to help a stranger's child."

The silence stretched out, filled only by the station's hissing breaths and Aino's own ragged attempts to stay calm.

She had not thought this through.

Had never considered that she wouldn't know where to hide.

Everything was in the open now, in this byway corridor on this big-cheese station.

All her life, there had always been another con, another mark, another chance to slip away and reinvent herself. Her parents had taught her that—how to be someone else when you needed to, how to tell a new story about who you were when the old one got you in trouble. But they'd never taught her what to do when there was nowhere left to run, because they'd never had that choice themselves. Their indenture contracts had decided everything.

"Maybe," Vera said finally, her voice barely audible, "maybe I was wrong about not wanting family. Maybe I just didn't want it with someone who would use it to control me."

Lin was quiet for a long moment. When she spoke again, her voice carried an odd note, something that might have been hope or might have been pain.

"The passport is in my office," she said. "I'll go get it."

Aino's head snapped up. Through her tears, she saw Vera's face transform with desperate relief. Now Vera was crying.

"Thank you," Vera breathed. "Lin, thank you, I—"

"In exchange," Lin continued, "you leave the girl with me."

All the air left the corridor. Marcus made a strangled sound, confusion in the twist of his eyebrows. Vera went very still. Her tears left tracks as they dried on her face.

Lin had never stopped looking at Aino.

"You want your freedom," Lin said. "And I want a family. She clearly needs somewhere to belong. This solves everyone's problem." The calm way Lin said it made everything ten times worse.

"No." Vera's voice was sharp. "She's a person, not a solution."

Lin moved closer to where Aino sat small against the wall, arms wrapped around her shins. "What happens when I turn her over to station security? She goes right back down-planet. Orphanage, or refugee camp. She's clearly been living rough—look at her clothes, her nails, her body. Good bones, but no fat at all."

Lin's voice had that particular tone adults used when they thought you couldn't understand—clinical, distant. Like Aino was a problem to solve instead of a person. The doctor smell was stronger now—that harsh soap that probably cost more than a week of meals, underlaid with something floral that made Aino's empty stomach turn. Rich people always smelled like flowers or fruit, like they were trying to prove they could waste money on smelling like food they'd never have to steal.

Aino felt the conversation flowing around her like water around a stone. Just like always, people deciding your life without even talking to you.

"Where exactly were you planning to take her?" Lin asked. "Or were you expecting her to run. Maybe even pointing out the route?"

"It wasn't like that," Vera sniffled, trying to sound offended.

In fact, it was exactly like that.

She was wrung out. Every bit of her, used up.

Go with the flow? Then at least she'd be solving someone else's "problem."

How humiliating.

"At least here she'd have medical care, education, a stable home," Lin continued. "I have a good position, a nice residential quarter. She could have your room! And a real childhood instead of whatever this is."

"And you get what you've always wanted," Vera said bitterly. "A ready-made family without having to negotiate with anybody about it."

Lin's lips trembled. "I don't want to be alone anymore, either. Not up here. And she'd be safe."

Aino closed her eyes, feeling the weight of that word. Safe. It sounded like prison walls and locked doors and someone else making every decision about her life. Like having to ask permission to pee. Like someone always watching when you ate. Like bedtimes and vegetables and *rules.*

But it also sounded like regular meals and warm clothes and not having to scan every room for exits and threats. Somebody who might wait up, worry if you came home late.

Lin crouched down in front of her, close

enough that Aino could smell her faint flowery perfume, read her name stitched in navy on the pocket of her doctor's coat, and see the tiny lines around her eyes. "I know you're not Emma Kellerman. I know you've been running a long time. Feels like you don't belong anywhere, right?"

She belonged at the elevator terminal, running the floor.

Except she didn't even belong there, anymore.

"I can make it so you belong here." Lin set a hand on Aino's knee. "What do you say?"

Aino studied Lin's face, trying to see her real, not through the mask of Aino's own exhaustion. This was a different kind of con. Like trading, but weird. Everyone was pretending they weren't trading. Like when kids swapped food but acted like they were just being nice so the monitors wouldn't stop them.

Lin wanted a child, Vera wanted her freedom.

And what did Aino want?

Food. Sleep.

To stop running.

Her hands started shaking. She lungs squeezed tight. She couldn't breathe.

She looked past Lin to Vera, who was watching with an expression of helpless frustration and something that might have been relief. They were all getting what they needed, just not the way any of them had planned.

Aino's chest felt too tight. She pressed harder against the wall, the cold metal the only thing that felt real. This was wrong. Everything about it was wrong. You didn't just... stop. You didn't just give up and let them catch you.

*Run,* the voice in her head screamed. The same voice that had kept her alive when the security dog had chased her through the terminals. The voice that sounded like her mom: *Never let them corner you, baby. There's always another way out.*

But her legs felt like water. When was the last time she'd really slept? Not just dozed in a maintenance closet with one ear open for footsteps, but actually *slept*? Her stomach cramped, remembering the half-eaten protein bar she'd fished from a trash bin this morning. Or was it yesterday?

"I don't need help," she said, but her voice came out small and cracked. She hated how young she sounded. "I'm fine on my own."

Lin stayed where she was. Smart. "I'm sure you are. How long since you've eaten a real meal?"

Aino's stomach answered before she could, growling loud enough that Marcus made a soft sound of sympathy. Aino's cheeks burned.

"I can take care of myself." The words were automatic, but even she could hear how tired they sounded. How many times had she said that? To social workers, to security guards, to other kids who tried to steal her food, her boots, her hiding spots.

*Get up, Get up and run. Break past them. There's always another way.*

But when she tried to push off the wall, her legs shook. Actually shook, like some little kid's. She slid back down, and this time she couldn't stop the tears. They came hot and angry and she hated them, hated being weak, hated that these strangers were seeing her like this.

"Hey," Vera said softly. She came closer, but not near Lin."It's okay. You've been so brave for so long. Maybe… maybe it's okay to let someone else be brave for you. Just for a little while."

*That's what they all say,* the survivor voice whispered. *Right before they lock you up*.

But another voice, quieter, asked: *What if she means it?*

"You want me to be your daughter," Aino said quietly.

"No," Lin said decisively. "You have parents, right?"

"Indentured. At Mining Colony Dexter 117."

Marcus gasped. "Way out there? And they just left you alone?"

"Shut up, Marcus," Vera said.

Lin just kept looking at her, with those round, brown, caring eyes. "So the corporation is holding your papers, right? So your parents will behave."

Marcus couldn't hold back. "They blackmail parents with their own kids?"

"Shut. Up."

"When's the indenture up?" Lin asked.

"Two years," Aino said through hiccups. "Supposed to be."

"So we could just try it out," Lin said. Her face went sad, a little lost. "I'll tell you a secret: I don't want to be alone, either. You'd really be helping me out."

For once, nobody was pretending to be an authority, or a guard, or an expert. They all were just figuring stuff out. Together.

Girl from Bennia Station. It was still a kind of performance, still a role to play. But this time, instead of pretending to be someone else's lost child, she could become someone's chosen child. Instead of stealing a life that didn't belong to her, she could build one that did. The choice felt strange in her mouth—bitter and sweet. Choosing something just because she wanted it.

She was so tired. Tired of running, tired of pretending, tired of always being one step away from disaster. The orbital station hummed around them, big and complicated and everything so strange. But maybe that meant it could become home to someone who had never really belonged anywhere.

Lin smiled, and for the first time it looked completely genuine. "And if you stay… what do you want to be called?"

The question made something crack inside Aino's chest. When was the last time anyone asked what *she* wanted? Not what name would fool the marks, not what identity would get her through security. Just… what she wanted.

Stay in one place. Be known. The idea felt like jumping off a cliff. Like that moment when you let go of one mag-lev cable before you've grabbed the next one, suspended over nothing but hope.

She wiped the tears off her face. "Aino."

"Aino. So, you'll stay?"

"Okay?" Her voice broke on the word.

*For now,* the survivor voice amended.

# ALSO BY NICKY PENTTILA

Cosmic Weave

*Cooperative Realm: Frankie's Journeys*

Cargo Trouble

Frankie Takes a Holiday

Frankie Takes a Dive

Frankie Finds a Dot

Frankie Takes a Bow

Cargo & Chaos: Frankie books 1 & 2

*Cooperative Realm: The Arkhide Chronicles*

Hidden Planet

The Listeners

The Elders of Arkhide

Tales of Arkhide story collection

*Short Stories*

Here: Earthbound Fantasies and Futures

There: Journeys to Imagined Realms

# ABOUT THE AUTHOR

Nicky Penttila wrote her first story, a Mayan murder mystery, in seventh grade. But then came gymnastics, math team, and boyfriends. Later came husband, car payments, and a sleep-depriving work schedule at newspapers across the country. Then came a second career as a science writer. But the fiction kept trickling out, a story here, a novella there, and finally, a real live novel. And she hasn't stopped.

Find more great reads at nickypenttila.com

www.ingramcontent.com/pod-product-compliance
Lightning Source LLC
LaVergne TN
LVHW050944080826
845145LV00004B/1401